GROSS GAMES

Y0-EIA-853

BY JANET HALFMANN
ILLUSTRATED BY MATT FOX

A GOLDEN BOOK®
Golden Books Publishing Company, Inc.
New York, New York 10106

1. A Slime Monster is hiding in a haunted house. He's ready to dump a bucket of slime on you. You can stop him if you can fit all the slimy words in the spaces.

GORY   GOO   GOOEY   ICKY
NASTY   OOZE   PUS   SLIME   SLUG
SPIT   STICKY   WORM

2. These hairy spiders need all their body parts so they can scare you. Fit the parts in the spaces—if you dare! The boxed letters will tell you what kind of spiders they are.

EIGHT LEGS   EYES   VENOM GLANDS
FANGS   THORAX   HEAD   SILK GLANDS
SILKY HAIR   MOUTH   JAWS

3. Can you get through the maze without getting caught in the spider's web?

START

FINISH

4. The skeleton's brew is missing one thing. To find out what it is, fill in the blanks with words that fit the clues. Then write the circled letters on the lines below and unscramble them.

Long thing at end of a rat. _ ◯ _ _

This is green and gooey. ◯ _ _ _ _

A snake flickers this. ◯ _ _ _ _ _

A very big spider. _ _ ◯ _ _ _ _ _ _

Yellow stuff in your ears. ◯ _ _

Letters: _ _ _ _ _

Answer: _ _ _ _ _

5. You're trapped in a haunted house with ghoulish monsters. The only way out is through the door with the big lock. Can you figure out the combination? Put the numbers 1 to 11 in the circles. Every set of 3 circles connected by a straight line must add up to 18. The 6 is already in place for you.

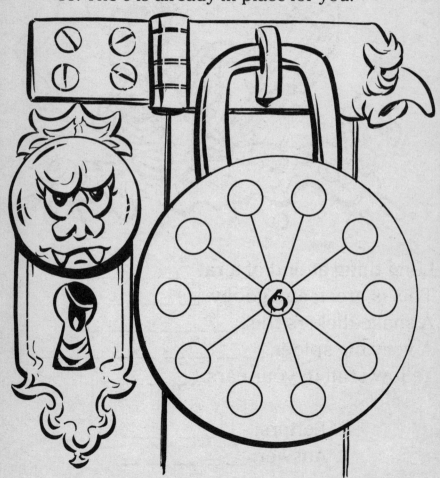

6. This mad scientist loves bugs—especially ones that bite, sting, or squirt nasty chemicals. Can you find all the bugs in the letter block before you become a target? Look up, down, forward, and backward.

ASSASSIN BUG BACK SWIMMER WASP
BOMBARDIER BEETLE BULLDOG ANT
CENTIPEDE FIRE ANT GIANT WATER BUG

```
F K L D B O X W E K
Q P N J O A N B D C
E A Q H M I B V E G
M R G Z B M C L P I
G Y P S A W P M I A
U S L T R U Q B T N
B U L L D O G A N T
N X K O I N D C E W
I S T G E F X K C A
S J N N R S R S V T
S P A E B E Y W J E
A R E D E H L I F R
S W R F E G I M S B
S I I Q T Z H M U U
A E F C L V A E T G
S N B A E R F R N T
```

7. What gross witch's stew ingredient is this witch giving out? Start at R and go clockwise around the cauldron twice. Write down every other letter and stop at T. Write the words on the lines.

___ _____

_____ ___

8. These three slimy creatures are leaving their homes to scare up some fun. Trace the slime trail between each creature and its home.

A.   B.   C.

1.   2.   3.

9. One of these ghoulish bugs is a gross-out. Find the one bug that contains all the letters in GROSS-OUT.

Use the gross code to find the answer to this riddle.

Why did the vampire enjoy art class?

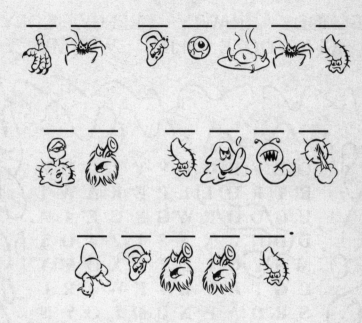

GROSS CODE

A	B	D	E	H	I

K	L	O	R	T	W

11. All these slimy words are hidden in the letter block—but they're in squiggly rather than straight lines. The words go in all directions, but letters in 1 word do not overlap letters in another word. The first one is done for you.

BLOODY   CRAWLY   CREEPY   GORY
ICKY   OOZE   SLIMY   WORMY

```
O E F B Q F Y Y I O H W
R T R H L L P E K A W T
U G O O R W G S C E I A
D D N C X A S I Z J O S
M S Y C Y D T L X O M Y
C G T R Y L I K W J R L
S R O A P N B M L O Y N
V L E E C A Y Z B M K A
```

12.

How many words can you make from the letters in GHOULISH ROTTEN BREW?

13. Use the code to figure out how many bats are in the belfry.

= 1   = 10   = 100

A. 8 + 6 + ___ = 20   **B.** 9 + ___ + 9 = 27

C. 6 - ___ + 15 = 19

D. 16 + 5 - 6 = ___

E. 100 + 39 - 4 = ___

14. Help keep this vampire happy. Using the clues, fill in the puzzle with the names of animals that drink blood.

ACROSS

1. Name sounds like "fright."
2. Two of these would be lice.
5. Flies at night.

DOWN

1. Humming pest of summer.
3. Makes dogs and cats itch.
4. Sleeps in bedding.

15. Follow the maze from head to foot.

FINISH

START

16.

Use the gross code to find the answer to this riddle.

What lies on the ground one hundred feet in the air?

____ ____ ____ ____ ____

____ ____ ____ ____ ____ ____ ____ ____ ____

GROSS CODE

A   C   D   E   I

N   P   T

17. Who will stop these creepy crawlies? Play this game with a friend. Take turns crossing out 1, 2, or 3 dots. The player who crosses out the last dot on a creepy crawly stops it—and is the winner.

18. Don't get grossed out. Can you find GROSS 16 times in this puzzle? Look up, down, forward, backward, and diagonally.

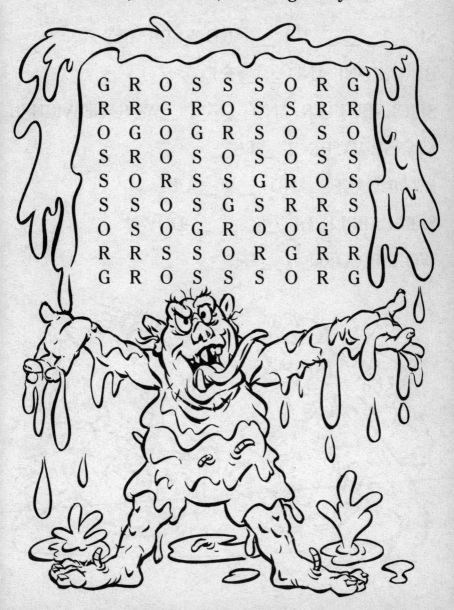

```
G R O S S S O R G
R R G R O S S R R
O G O G R S O R O
S R O S O S O S S
S O R S S G R O S
S S O S G S R R S
O S O G R O O G O
R R S S O R G R R
G R O S S S O R G
```

19. Two monsters are planning a ghoulish party. Can you finish the words to help them?

SP _ _ _ _ T T _ AND EYEBALLS

BUGARONI AND _ _ E E _ _

SPIDERBUTTER AND _ _ L _ Y SANDWICHES

MARSHWATER T _ FF _

BRAINCAKES AND _ Y _ UP

SLIMEAPPLE UP_ _ _ _-DOWN _ A _ _

WORMYCORN B _ L L _

20. What is the grossest creature you can imagine? Draw it here.

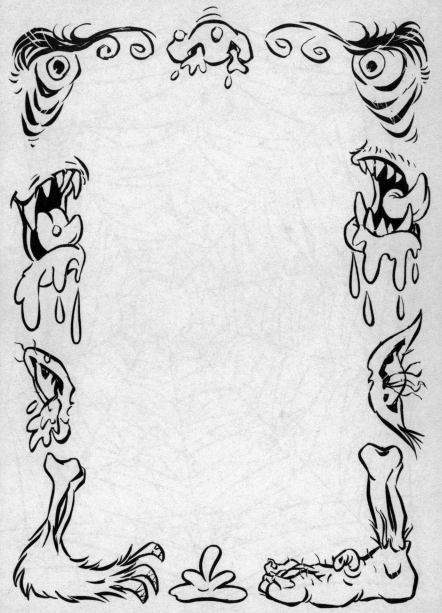

21. Lots of spiders are hiding and waiting to scare you. How many can you count?

22. How many words can you make from the letters in SWAMP SLIME SLUDGE?

23. Use the gross code to find the answer to this riddle.

WHY IS A SKELETON SUCH A SCAREDY-CAT?

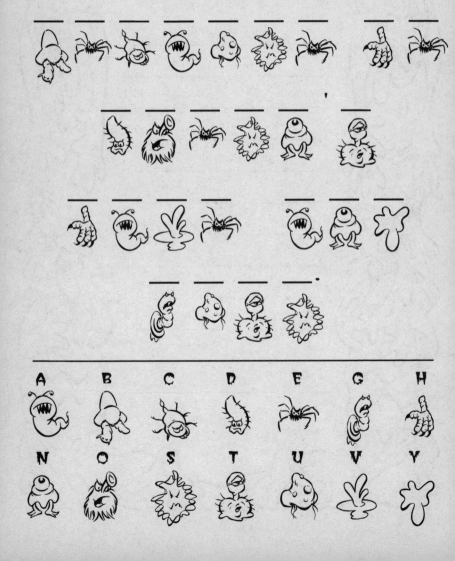

24. A rattlesnake's bite is worse than its rattle! How many complete snakes are hidden in this puzzle? Trace each one from its rattle to its head to find out.

25. Take turns with a friend drawing a straight line between 2 dots to make a square. As you complete a square, initial it and take another turn. Count 2 points for each square with a creature and 1 point for each of the others. The player with the most points wins.

26. How much do you know about the creatures of gross brews and potions? Circle True or False for each item.

1. Only male mosquitoes bite.   T   F
2. All insects have six legs.   T   F
3. A flea can jump 200 times the length of its body.   T   F
4. The vampire bat eats insects and fruit.   T   F
5. Cockroaches are smart enough to run through a maze.   T   F
6. The fire ant's sting burns like fire.   T   F
7. The scorpion stings with its pincers.   T   F
8. All spiders have six legs.   T   F
9. The fangs of snakes are special teeth used to inject poison.   T   F
10. Tarantulas seldom bite human beings.   T   F

27. Add letters from the word GROSS to finish this ghoulish menu.

APPETIZER: Veggie V__mit

SOUP: C__ck__ __ach S__up

MAIN COURSE: T__asted T__ngues

SALAD: B__ ain Cell __alad

SIDE DISH: W__ __my Baked Apple __

DRINK: __aliva __lu__p

DESSERT: Lice C__eam

28. What ghoulish dishes would you serve to a gross gourmet? Write your creations on the lines.

APPETIZER: _____

SOUP: _____

MAIN COURSE: _____

SALAD: _____

SIDE DISH: _____

DRINK: _____

DESSERT: _____

29. Now draw some of your ghoulishly gross gourmet foods.

30. To find a gross tongue twister, first solve the math problems. Then insert the correct letters in the puzzle. The first one is done for you.

CODE:

12	18	24	30	36	42	48	54	60	66	72	78
L	P	R	S	Y	D	I	M	E	U	O	W

45 −15	9 +9	12 x4	7 x6	30 +30	6 x4	60 −30
30	**18**	**48**	**42**	**60**	**24**	**30**
S	P	I	D	E	R	S

18 +12	18 −6	11 x6	36 −12	30 −12
☐	☐	☐	☐	☐

6 x5	20 −8	50 −2	6 x3	16 +2	12 x5	13 +11	24 +12
☐	☐	☐	☐	☐	☐	☐	☐

30 −0	6 +6	8 x6	9 x6	100 −40
☐	☐	☐	☐	☐

15 +15	4 x3	9 x8	60 +18	9 +3	6 x6
☐	☐	☐	☐	☐	☐

31. Follow the numbers in the boxes and draw the art in the right order to see something gross.

32. Can you trace a path through the trash and garbage?

START

FINISH

33. Can you find 15 ghoulish monsters hidden in the cemetery before they find you?

34. Want to taste this homemade maggot stew? Unscramble the words to see what's in it.

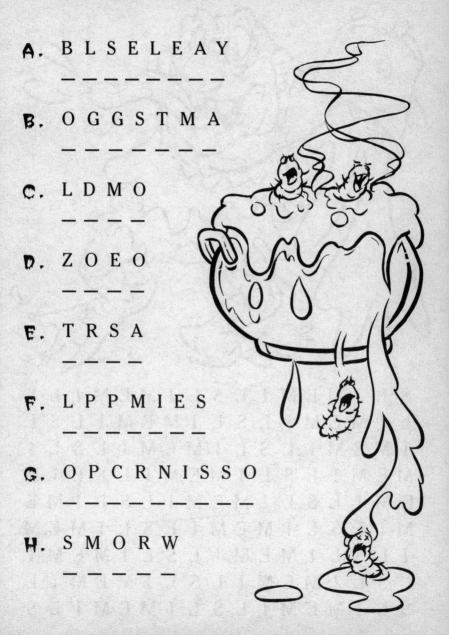

A. B L S E L E A Y

_ _ _ _ _ _ _ _

B. O G G S T M A

_ _ _ _ _ _ _ _

C. L D M O

_ _ _ _

D. Z O E O

_ _ _ _

E. T R S A

_ _ _ _

F. L P P M I E S

_ _ _ _ _ _ _ _

G. O P C R N I S S O

_ _ _ _ _ _ _ _ _

H. S M O R W

_ _ _ _ _

35. This puzzle has been slimed. Can you find SLIME 52 times?

```
S L I M E M I L S L I M E M I L S
L I M E M I L S L I M E M I L S L
I M E M I L S L I M E M I L S L I
M E M I L S L I M E M I L S L I M
E M I L S L I M E M I L S L I M E
M I L S L I M E M I L S L I M E M
I L S L I M E M I L S L I M E M I
L S L I M E M I L S L I M E M I L
S L I M E M I L S L I M E M I L S
```

36. To find the answer to the riddle below, fit all the ghostly words in the spaces. The boxed letters will answer the riddle.

WHAT DO YOU CALL A SKELETON THAT SLEEPS LATE IN THE MORNING?

SPIDERS   WEB   POTION   BATS   SCARY
WIZARD   MAGIC   GHOULS   MOON

37. Find a skeleton in this picture.

38. These spiders want to run their fastest—to better scare everyone they see! But they're each missing some legs. Add legs so each spider has 8.

39. Ick! Find your way through this maze by following the path that spells GROSS-OUT.

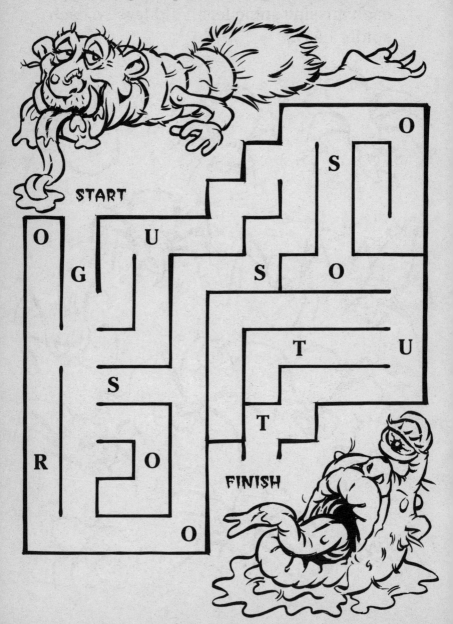

40. Circle True or False for each item.

1. A rattlesnake has a rattle on its head. T F
2. Frogs and toads have long sticky tongues. T F
3. Two of the most dangerous spiders are the black widow and the brown recluse. T F
4. Centipedes have 1,000 legs. T F
5. Millipedes do not bite. T F
6. A slug's slime is so protective that it can climb over a sharp knife unharmed. T F
7. A fly tastes with its feet. T F
8. The brown rat is the biggest rat in the world. T F
9. In the past, doctors sometimes used leeches to suck their patients' blood. T F
10. The bombardier beetle squirts out a nasty gas that makes a frog gag. T F

41. The Ghoulish Monsters are cooking again. Help them finish the names of these ghastly dishes.

HARD-BO__ __ __ D SLUGS

FRUIT FLY P__ __ C H

CHO__ __ __ __ TE BRAINSHAKE

HO __ RAT AND CATSUP

COCKROACH CH__P C__ __KIES

FLEAS-IN-A-BL__ __KET

RO __ __ T TOAD SANDWICH

C __ ICK __ N COBWEB S__UP

42. There's a message on the tombstone, but it's in code. To read it, move the first letter of each word to the end.

EWELCOM,
SGHOUL
DAN
SGOBLIN.
EHAV
A
VSLIM
VDA.

43. It's a gross haunted house! Can you find 9 things grossly wrong in this picture?

44. Stop the centipedes. Put + and – signs in each problem so all the answers equal 100.

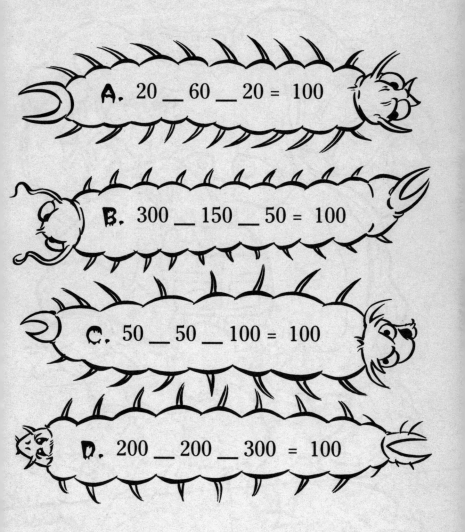

A. 20 __ 60 __ 20 = 100

B. 300 __ 150 __ 50 = 100

C. 50 __ 50 __ 100 = 100

D. 200 __ 200 __ 300 = 100

45. Find 5 spiders hidden in the dirty clothes hamper.

46. Lead the monster to the treats. To find the path, start at the word PAW. Move across or down, but only to spaces with words made from the letters in CREEPY and CRAWLY.

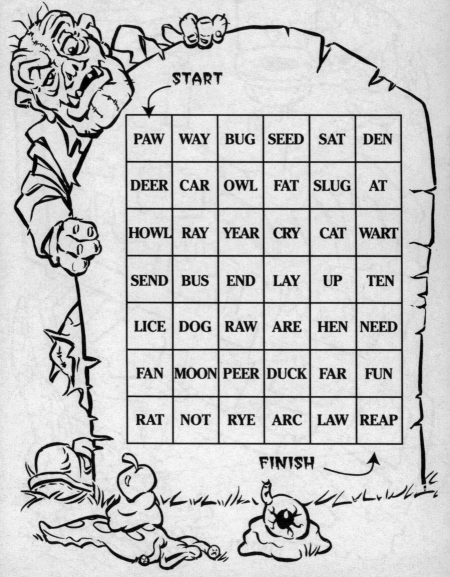

START

PAW	WAY	BUG	SEED	SAT	DEN
DEER	CAR	OWL	FAT	SLUG	AT
HOWL	RAY	YEAR	CRY	CAT	WART
SEND	BUS	END	LAY	UP	TEN
LICE	DOG	RAW	ARE	HEN	NEED
FAN	MOON	PEER	DUCK	FAR	FUN
RAT	NOT	RYE	ARC	LAW	REAP

FINISH

47. Help the baby alligator find his way back to his mama through the sewer system!

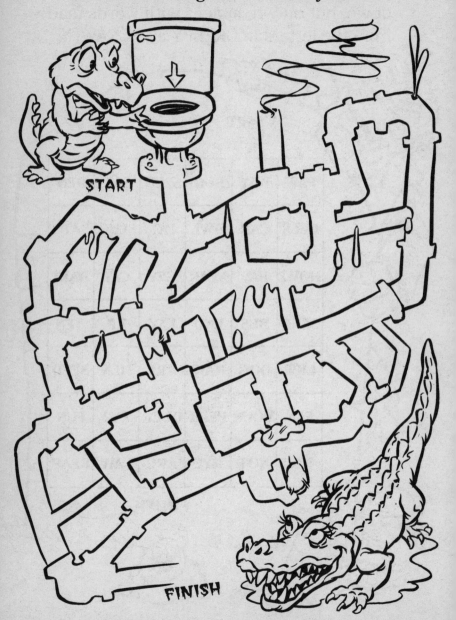

START

FINISH

48. Find these scary words. Look up, down, forward, backward, and diagonally.

WORD LIST:

BATS BREW BONES CAT COBWEBS
COSTUME CREAK CREEPY EEK FLEA
HAUNTED MASK MOON OWL RAT ROACHES
SKELETON SNAKE TOADS WEREWOLF WITCH

```
C O S T U M E D B
W I T C H B R E W
N O O M C A T T E
S K E L E T O N R
B O N E S S A U E
E O R O K T D A W
W K S A M A S H O
B A E L F R N H L
O R O A C H E S F
C R E E P Y L W O
```

49. Even monsters bite their nails! Put these gruesome hands back together by matching the correct nails to the hands.

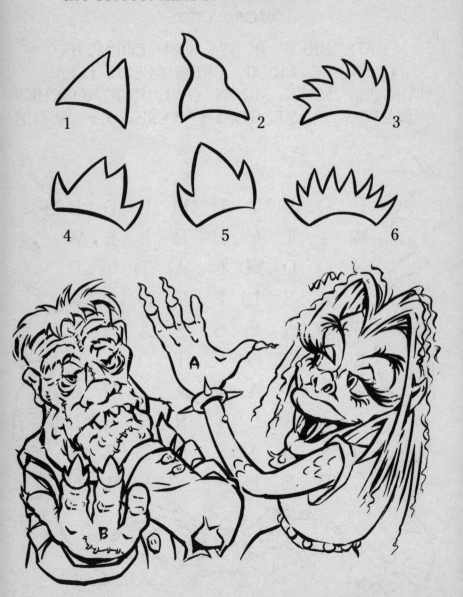

50. The mad scientist needs one more thing for his potion. To find out what it is, fill in the blanks with the words that fit the clues. Then write the circled letters on the line below and unscramble them.

A. A snail leaves a trail of

_ _ _ _ (_) .

B. Vampire bats have sharp

_ _ _ _ (_) .

C. _ _ _ (_) _ or treat.

D. Vampires drink _ (_) _ _ _ .

E. A centipede has up to 100

_ (_) _ _ .

LETTERS: _ _ _ _ _

ANSWER: _ _ _ _ _ _

51. Find the centipede that is different.

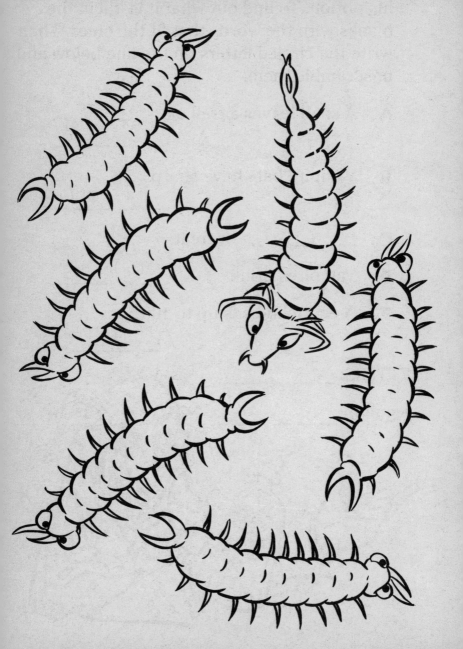

52. To find the answer to this riddle, cross out all the numbers.

WHAT BUG CAN HELP YOU WITH YOUR MATH HOMEWORK?

1291T973H841E639986

A248R632I734T539H624M96E3

9564T2678I73C692K2865

53. Find the SHORTEST path through the maze to escape the monster.

Can you find all the creatures haunting this house?

55. Help the pigs find the way through their disgusting pen to their bucket of slop.

56. The wizard wants to make some brew, but his helper brought all the wrong ingredients. Can you change the following things into proper ingredients for a ghoulish brew? The first one is done for you.

A. STAR   <u>R</u>   <u>A</u>   <u>T</u>   <u>S</u>

B. STRAW   __ __ __ __ __

C. LEAF   __ __ __ __

D. TIPS   __ __ __ __

E. NAILS   __ __ __ __ __

F. LIMES   __ __ __ __ __

57. These bugs are getting ready to corner you. Here's how you can stop them: Connect them using only 4 lines. You must keep your pencil on the paper, and you must not pass through any bug more than once.

58. Lots of creatures are scurrying through the sewage plant. Can you tell who they are by how many legs they have? Use the clues to fit their names in the puzzle.

ACROSS

1. 6 legs; rhymes with mice (plural)
4. 8-legged big, hairy spider
5. 8-legged web builder
7. 2-legged bird; has wise eyes
9. 8 legs, 2 pincers, and a stinger

DOWN

2. Up to 100 legs
3. 4 legs; has warts
5. No legs; leaves a slime trail
6. 4 legs; rhymes with cat
7. 8 arms; lives in the sea
8. 6 legs; lives in a colony

59.

Use the gross code to find the answer to this riddle.

WHAT DRIVES A CENTIPEDE CRAZY?

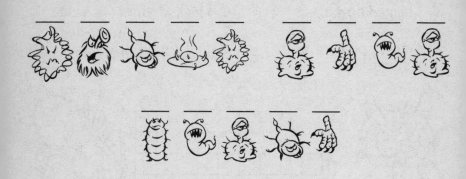

GROSS CODE

ANSWER PAGES

1. STICKY, SLUG, ICKY, SLIME, GOOEY, WORM, GOO, NASTY, PUS, SPIT, OOZE, GORY

2.
```
            THORAX
          JAWS
SILKY HAIR
  VENOM GLANDS
        FANGS
    EIGHT LEGS
        MOUTH
        SILK GLANDS
        HEAD
      EYES
```

3.

4. TAIL, SLIME, TONGUE, TARANTULA, WAX
Letters: A, S, T, R, W
Answer: WARTS

5.

6.

7. RED ROASTED ROTTEN RAT

8. A-3; B-1; C-2

9.

10. HE LIKED TO DRAW BLOOD.

11.

12. Possible answers: BEE, BET, BIG, BIT, BITE, BITTEN, BOG, BONE, BOO, BOOT, BOWL, BOWLING, BRIGHT, BUG, GET, GHOST, GHOUL, GIRL, GLOB, GLOW, GO, GONE, GOON, GORE, GOT, GOWN, GREEN, GREW, GRIN, GROW, GUTS, HE, HEN, HIT, HOG, HOLE, HOOT, HORN, HORSE, HOT, HOUSE, HOW, HOWL, HUG, LEG, LET, LETTER, LIST, LOG, LOST, LOT, LOW, LOWER, RELISH, RIG, RIGHT, ROB, ROBE, ROLE, ROT, ROW, RUG, SEW, SHEET, SHORT, SHOUT, SHUT, SO, SOLE, SON, SORE, SOUR, SHORE, THROB, THROUGH, TIGHT, TONIGHT, TOUGH, TOUR, TOW, TOWN, TROUGH, WEB, WET, WHITE, WHO, WHOLE, WIG, WON, WORE

13. A. 6; B. 9; C. 2; D. 15; E. 135

14.

15.

16. A DEAD CENTIPEDE

18.

G	R	O	S	S	(S)	S	O	R	G
R		R	G	R	O	S	S	R	R
O	G	O	G	R	S	O		O	O
S		R	O	S	O	S		R	S
S	R		S	S	G	R		S	S
(S)	O	R	S	O	S	S	R		(S)
S		S	O	G	R	O	O		O
R	R	S	S	O	R	G	R		R
G	R	O	S	(S)	S	O	R	G	

19. SPAGHETTI AND EYEBALLS,
BUGARONI AND CHEESE,
SPIDERBUTTER AND JELLY
SANDWICHES, MARSHWATER
TAFFY, BRAINCAKES AND SYRUP,
SLIMEAPPLE UPSIDE-DOWN
CAKE, WORMYCORN BALLS

21. 14

22. Possible answers: AGE, AMPLE,
DAMP, DEEP, DIAL, DIG, DIM,
DIME, DULL, GAME, GEM,
GLADE, GLASS, GLEAM, GLUE,
GLUM, GUESS, LAMP, LAP, LAW,
LEAP, LED, LEDGE, LESS, LID,
LIME, LIMP, MAD, MADE, MAIL,
MALE, MALL, MASS, MAP, MILE,
MISS, MUD, PAD, PAGE, PAL,
PALE, PASS, PAW, PEG, PIG, PILE,
PLUS, PUS, SAGE, SAID, SAIL,
SALE, SAME, SAP, SAW, SEEP,

SIDE, SLED, SLEEP, SLID, SLIDE,
SLUG, SWAP, WAG, WAGE, WALL,
WEDGE, WELL, WIDE, WILD,
WILL, WISE

23. BECAUSE HE DOESN'T HAVE
ANY GUTS.

24. 6

26. 1. F (Only female mosquitoes
bite; they need blood for their
eggs.); 2. T; 3. T; 4. F (Most bats
eat insects and fruit, but the
vampire bat drinks blood.); 5. T;
6. T; 7. F (It stings with its tail.);
8. F (A spider is not an insect;
it is an arachnid and therefore
has 8 legs.); 9. T; 10. T

27. VEGGIE VOMIT, COCKROACH
SOUP, TOASTED TONGUES,
BRAIN CELL SALAD, WORMY
BAKED APPLES, SALIVA SLURP,
LICE CREAM

30. SPIDERS SLURP SLIPPERY SLIME
SLOWLY

31.

32.

33.

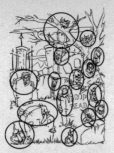

34. EYEBALLS, MAGGOTS, MOLD, OOZE, RATS, PIMPLES, SCORPIONS, WORMS

35.

```
S L I M E M I L S S L I M E M I L S
L I M E M I L S S L I M E M I L S L
I M E M I L S S L I M E M I L S L I
M E M I L S S L I M E M I L S L I M
E M I L S S L I M E M I L S L I M E
M I L S S L I M E M I L S L I M E M
I L S S L I M E M I L S L I M E M I
L S S L I M E M I L S L I M E M I L
S L I M E M I L S S L I M E M I L S
```

36.

```
G H O U L S
    M A G I C
    W I Z A R D
S C A R Y
        B A T S
      P O T I O N
M O O N
      W E B
      S P I D E R S
```

37.

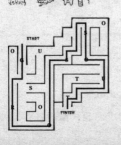

39.

40. 1. F (The rattle is on its tail.); 2. T; 3. T; 4. F (Centipedes have up to 100 legs; millipedes have more, but not the 1000 that their name implies.); 5. T; 6. T; 7. T; 8. F (The cane rat is the largest at 20 pounds.); 9. T; 10. T

41. HARD-BOILED SLUGS, FRUIT FLY PUNCH, CHOCOLATE BRAINSHAKE, HOT RAT AND CATSUP, COCKROACH CHIP COOKIES, FLEAS-IN-A-BLANKET, ROAST TOAD SANDWICH, CHICKEN COBWEB SOUP

42. WELCOME, GHOULS AND GOBLINS. HAVE A SLIMY DAY.

43.

44. 1. 20 + 60 + 20 = 100
2. 300 - 150 - 50 = 100
3. 50 - 50 + 100 = 100
4. 200 + 200 - 300 = 100

45.

46.

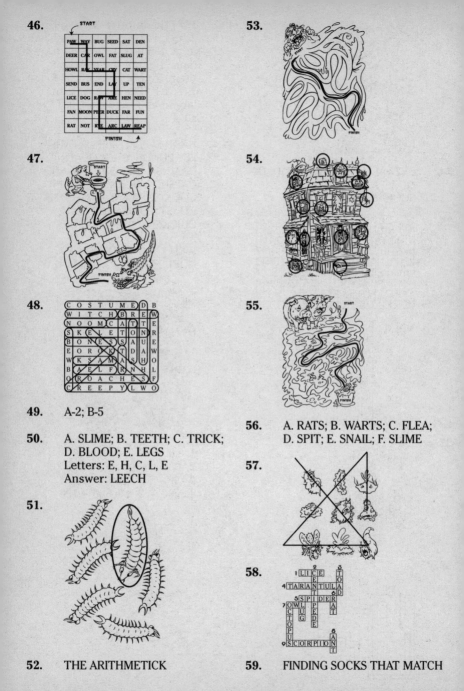

START

PAW	WAY	BUG	SEED	SAT	DEN
DEER	CAR	OWL	FAT	SLUG	AT
HOWL	RAT	YEAR	CRY	CAT	WART
SEND	BUS	END	LAY	UP	TEN
LICE	DOG	RAW	ARE	HEN	NEED
FAN	MOON	PEER	DUCK	FAR	FUN
RAT	NOT	RYE	ARC	LAW	REAP

FINISH

47.

START

FINISH

48.

C O S T U M E D B
W I T C H B R E W
N O O M C A T T E
S K E L E T O N R
B O N E S S A U E
E O R O K T D A W
W K S A M T R N O
A E L M A U H L F
O R O A C H E S F
C R E E P Y L W O

49. A-2; B-5

50. A. SLIME; B. TEETH; C. TRICK;
D. BLOOD; E. LEGS
Letters: E, H, C, L, E
Answer: LEECH

51.

52. THE ARITHMETICK

53.

START

FINISH

54.

55.

START

FINISH

56. A. RATS; B. WARTS; C. FLEA;
D. SPIT; E. SNAIL; F. SLIME

57.

58.

L I C E T O A D
T A R A N T U L A
O W L S P I D E R A T
C U G P
T E E D
O D E
P
U
S C O R P I O N A N T

59. FINDING SOCKS THAT MATCH